D0065052

I SEE A SIGN

to Richard Hackel

Text and photographs copyright © 1996 by Lars Klove

Simon & Schuster Books for Young Readers
An imprint of Simon & Schuster Children's Publishing Division
1230 Avenue of the Americas
New York, NY 10020

READY-TO-READ is a registered trademark of Simon & Schuster, Inc.

Also available in an Aladdin Paperbacks Edition.

The text of this book was set in Utopia.

Printed and bound in the United States of America

10 9 8 7 6 5 4 3 2 1

The Library of Congress has cataloged the Simon & Schuster Books
for Young Readers edition as follows:
Klove, Lars.
I see a sign / written and illustrated by Lars Klove.
p. cm.—(Ready-to-Read)
Summary: Describes a variety of signs telling you where to shop, eat,
and find people, places, and things.
1. Signs and symbols—Juvenile literature. [1. Signs and symbols.]
I. Title. II. Series.
P99.K564 1996
302.238—dc20   95-50867
CIP   AC
ISBN 0-689-80800-3 (hc) 0-689-80799-6 (pbk)

I SEE A SIGN

Written and illustrated by Lars Klove

Ready-to-Read

Simon & Schuster Books for Young Readers

TO THE READER:

You may think of reading as something you do with books. But you are reading all the time. At home, you read notes and cereal boxes and soup cans. When you are outside, you can read signs.

This book will show you some of the signs you can read. The signs tell you where to shop, eat, and where to find people, places, and things. Look for them the next time you go outside. You'll see some of the signs in this book and many other signs that you can read.

Signs tell you
when to stop...

stop

don't walk

and when to go,

wait

and which way to go

out

and where to go.

Main Street

Fruit Street

dead end

They also tell you where not to go.

Some signs tell you where the entrance is.

enter here

Some help you find the exit.

exit

corn

fresh fish daily

fruits

brown eggs

pick your own

Signs show you where to buy the food you eat at home.

honey for sale

pizza

homemade soup
fresh daily

cold drinks

milk, juice, and dairy
we sell ice cream
fresh fruits and vegetables

hot dogs 500 feet

special! four donuts $1.00

take-out

restaurant
breakfast, lunch, dinner

fresh warm cookies

If you eat out, they show you where to get your breakfast, lunch, dinner, and snacks.

barber

After you've eaten, you can find
a place to cut your hair,
or hide it with a hat

hats

wigs

or a wig that's green or orange or white.

flat fixed
used rim and tire

If your car has a flat tire, you can get it fixed.

16

bikes

flat fix

shoe repair

You can ride a bike,
or fix your old
shoes and walk.

school

slow: children

slow: cat crossing

deer crossing

bike crossing

While you're on your way, watch out
for children, cats, deer, bikes, and. . .

railroad crossing

...trains.

How many railroad cars can you count?

one

two

three

four

five

six

seven

eight

nine

ten

Some signs can help you count. They don't have any words at all.

If you need to be by yourself,
look for a place that's quiet.

quiet zone

books

flowers

toys

If you want to give a gift, look for a place to buy flowers, a book, or a toy.

Sometimes signs have warnings.

danger

bump

wet paint

hard hat area

Ignore them at your own risk!

fire

fire station

fire patrol number one

hook and ladder

26

police department, city of New York

police

help wanted

Signs tell you where to go if you need help and where you can be of help.

ice

Some signs have pictures that
tell you what they say.

28

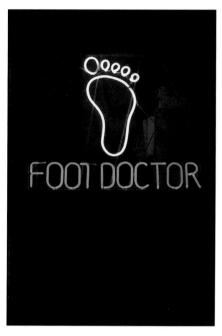

we make keys   **foot doctor**

repair it here

Be careful! Sometimes the pictures in the signs are tricky.

**garden worms
lures, rods, reels**

Or the sign doesn't match what's in the window.

repairs

Look down below you. The words on manholes tell you what is in the pipes that run under city streets.

tree water

gas

drain

water

31

cats, kittens for adoptions

free kittens

And sometimes, a sign can tell you where to find a friend.

**PLEASE DO NOT REMOVE
DATE DUE CARD FROM POCKET**

By returning material on date due, you will help
us save the cost of postage for overdue notices.
We hope you enjoy the library. Come again and
bring your friends!

FALMOUTH PUBLIC LIBRARY
Falmouth, Mass. 02540-2895
508-457-2555

DEMCO